Barbie™
VIDEO GAME™
HERO™ #1

Need For Speed

PAPERCUTZ™

MORE GREAT GRAPHIC NOVEL SERIES AVAILABLE FROM PAPERCUTZ

BARBIE #1

BARBIE PUPPY PARTY

BARBIE #2

BARBIE STARLIGHT ADVENTURE

FUZZY BASEBALL

THE GARFIELD SHOW #6

DISNEY FAIRIES #18

MINNIE & DAISY #1

NANCY DREW DIARIES #7

THE RED SHOES

SCARLETT

THE SISTERS #1

THE WILD SMURF

THEA STILTON #6

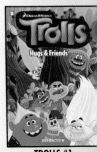
TROLLS #1

Barbie VIDEO GAME HERO #1

Story by Tini Howard
Art by Jules Rivera

PAPERCUTZ

NEW YORK

BARBIE VIDEO GAME HERO #1 "Need for Speed"

Tini Howard – Writer
Jules Rivera – Artist
Laurie Smith – Colorist (cover)
Ronda Pattison – Colorist
Janice Chiang – Letterer

Grace Ilori – Production
Mariah McCourt – Editor
Jeff Whitman - Assistant Managing Editor
Beth Scorzato – Special Thanks
Jim Salicrup
Editor-in-Chief

Papercutz books may be purchased for business or promotional use. For information on bulk purchases please contact Macmillan Corporate and Premium Sales Department at (800) 221-7945 x5442.

ISBN: 978-162991-644-6 hardcover edition
ISBN: 978-162991-643-9 paperback edition

Printed in China
September 2017

Distributed by Macmillan
First Printing

6

--WHO WILL BE THE WINNER OF THIS RACE BETWEEN FRIENDS?!

THAT WAS *FUN!* GREAT RACE, BELLA.

SO, WHO *WON?*

IN A RACE THAT FINISHED SIDE BY SIDE, WOULD YOU BELIEVE IT WAS A *TIE!*

REMATCH, BARBIE?

WAIT, WHERE'S *KRIS?*

GUESS HIS SHORTCUT WASN'T AS *SUCCESSFUL* AS HE THOUGHT.

IT'S ON! LET'S FIND THE WHOLE TEAM AND MEET UP IN THE CENTRAL PORTAL!

WE'LL MEET YOU THERE, CUTIE!

LET'S DO IT!

HANG IN THERE, *KRIS*-- WE'LL BE BACK FOR YOU!

I HOPE HE'S OKAY!

MEANWHILE...

WOOOO-HOO!

WOW, THIS LEVEL IS GREAT! I GUESS IT WASN'T WHERE I WAS TRYING TO GO, BUT...

SURE IS *FUN!*

...I HOPE NO ONE IS *LOOKING* FOR ME...

BARBIE! BELLA! CUTIE!

IT'S SO GOOD TO SEE YOU ALL!

DID YOU COME FOR THE PICNIC? WE JUST GOT STARTED!

I WISH! CRYSTAL, HAVE YOU SEEN ANYTHING WEIRD?

NOPE! EVERYTHING OKAY?

KRIS, BELLA, AND I WERE RACING AT THE BOARDWALK AND NOW KRIS IS GONE!

GONE?

BARBIE FOUND A BREAK IN THE LEVEL'S CODE! IF WE GATHER OUR FRIENDS, WE CAN SAVE KRIS FROM THE HOLE!

OH--

CENTRAL PORTAL. THE TEAM'S SECRET HEADQUARTERS.

OKAY, TEAM, PIPE IN WITH YOUR IDEAS!

CAN YOU CODE A PROJECTION OF THE BOARDWALK, SO WE CAN SEE IT?

AND MAYBE SOME SNACKS?

DONE AND... *DONE!*

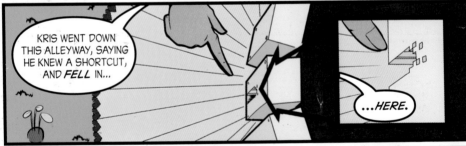

KRIS WENT DOWN THIS ALLEYWAY, SAYING HE KNEW A SHORTCUT, AND *FELL* IN...

...HERE.

KRIS KNEW ABOUT THE SHORTCUT, BUT DID HE KNOW ABOUT THE HOLE?

THAT'S A GOOD POINT. BELLA?

GOSH, I DON'T THINK SO.

IF IT HADN'T BEEN THERE, HE WOULD HAVE COME OUT BY WHERE OUR RACE ENDS. I DON'T THINK HE WAS *TRYING* TO GO THERE.

THERE'S NO ONE FASTER THAN US. IF WE CAN GET IN THERE, WE CAN PULL HIM OUT!

IF WE CAN FIND HIM...

LET'S HIT THE *BOARDWALK* AND FIND OUT!

THIS PLACE GOT CROWDED!

WHAT'S EVERYONE LOOKING AT?

OH, NO...

THE HOLE IN THE CODE IS CONTINUING TO GROW! IF ANYONE ELSE CAME THIS WAY-- OH, NO!

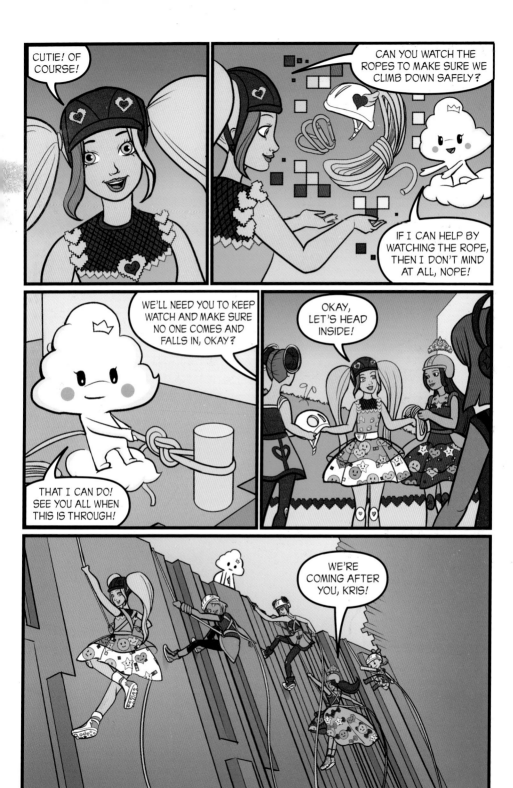

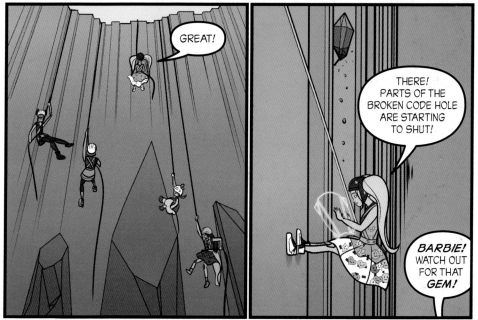

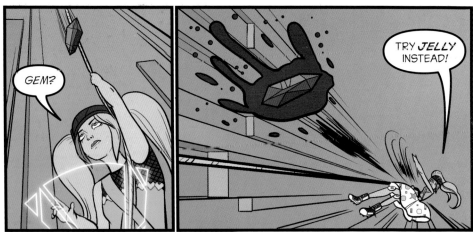

YEAH, WE'RE GETTING CLOSER--

OH!

BWOOP

GEEZ! OR MAYBE WE'RE NOT!

I THINK WE ARE...

...BUT THIS IS WHERE THE GAME KEEPS THINGS THAT AREN'T QUITE RIGHT!

IT USUALLY *ISN'T!*

BUT THIS IS THE DE-BUG ROOM...

SO *WHAT* DO WE DO?

I HAVE THE *PERFECT* POWER-UP...

YOU'VE HEARD OF BUG SPRAY?

THIS IS DE-BUG SPRAY!

WE *DEBUG* IT!

FWSSSSST

THERE WE GO! NOW THEY'RE NOT *BUGS,* THEY'RE LOVELY *BUTTERFLIES!*

WELL, IF WE'RE GOING IN THE RIGHT WAY...

...WHAT ARE WE *WAITING* FOR?

LET'S FIND KRIS!

KRA-KOOM

WHOA!

THAT...*WAS* UNEXPECTED.

NO KIDDING! THIS IS A REALLY *HIGH LEVEL*--WE MUST HAVE SKIPPED TO IT FROM THE DEBUG ROOM!

THOSE HOLES ALL OPEN TO *NEW LEVELS.*

GRACKLE

GRACKLE

KRAK

KRA A

KROOM

EEP!

OKAY, I'M *OUT* OF IDEAS. WHAT DO *WE* DO?

I CAN'T *CODE* THE LIGHTNING--

IT'S TOO FAST! NOT EVEN *I* CAN CODE THAT FAST.

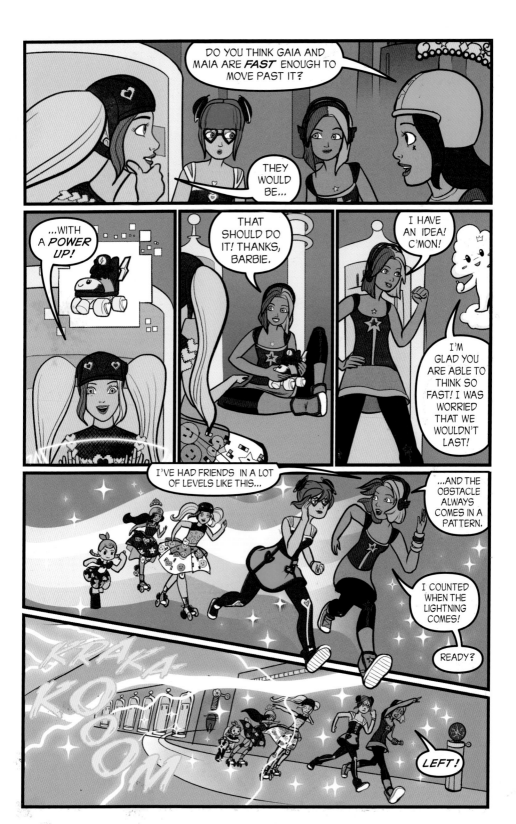

REALLY? ALL THIS WAY, JUST TO GET STOPPED BY A PILE OF *JUNK?*

HMM, THESE MUST BE ITEMS THEY WROTE INTO THE CODE, AND THEN DIDN'T NEED! THEY JUST *LEAVE* THEM IN THIS OLD JUNK FOLDER.

SO WHAT DO WE DO WITH ALL THIS JUNK?

SHOVE IT ASIDE?

WE CAN'T JUST SHOVE IT ASIDE...WE'LL HAVE TO *CLEAN* IT UP. THE GOOD NEWS IS, IF YOU ALL HELP ME ORGANIZE THE CODE, WE CAN MAKE IT A *GAME!*

YOU KNOW I *LOVE* A GOOD GAME!

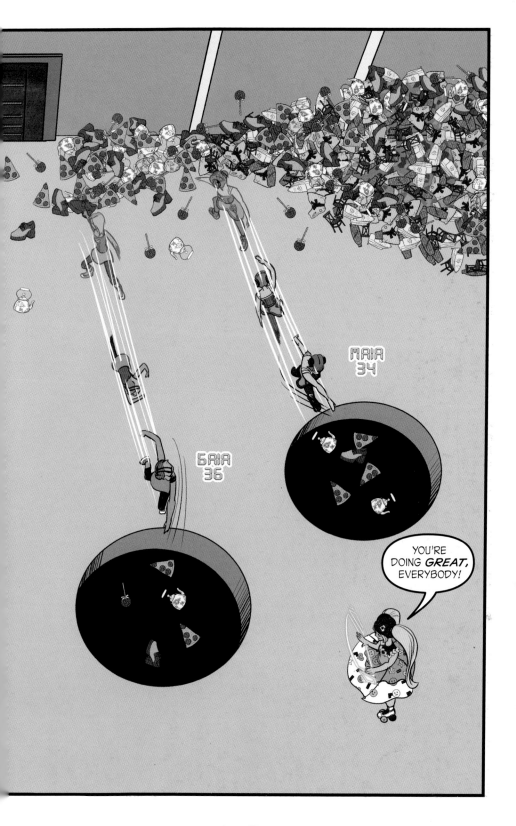

THIS IS SO STRANGE-- A COMPLETELY FINISHED LEVEL?

ON OUR JOURNEY, BARBIE, THIS IS THE LAST LEG-- THIS LEVEL YOU'VE FOUND IS AN EASTER EGG!

EASTER EGG?

I DON'T SEE ANY EASTER EGGS. IT'S NOT EVEN SPRING!

NO, SILLY!

AN EASTER EGG IS A SPECIAL PART OF A VIDEO GAME THAT IS A SECRET TO BE DISCOVERED!

WHEN YOU FELL INTO THE BROKEN CODE, YOU MUST HAVE BOUNCED AROUND BEFORE LANDING HERE!

OH...I THOUGHT THAT **WAS** THE SHORTCUT!

I SAW IT DAYS AGO AND DIDN'T KNOW WHAT IT WAS, I THOUGHT IT MIGHT BE A SECRET PASSAGE?

AND IT WAS! JUST... NOT TO THE END OF THE BOARDWALK.

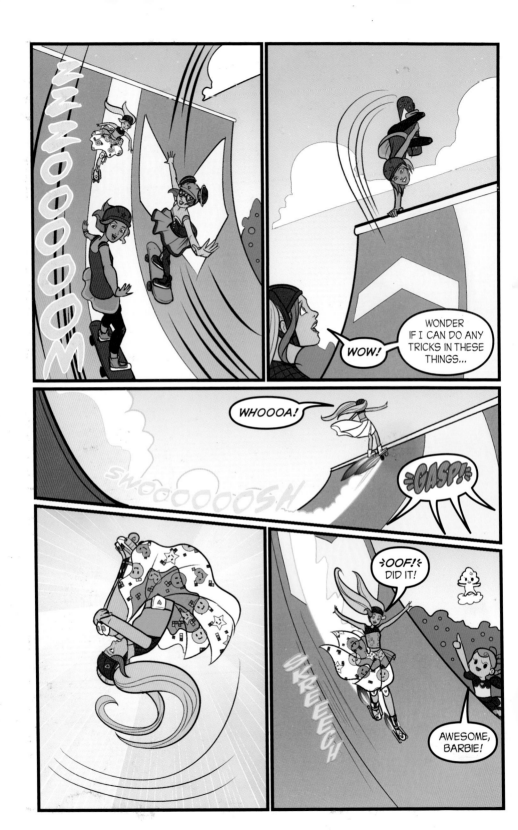

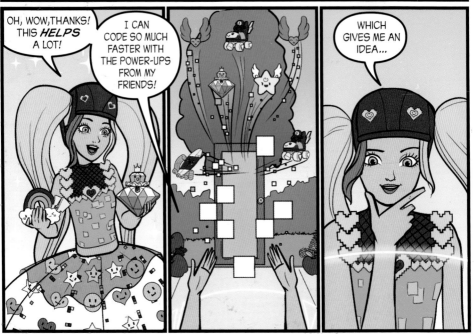

WATCH OUT FOR PAPERCUTZ

Welcome to the fast-paced, premiere BARBIE VIDEO GAME HERO graphic novel from Papercutz, for those fashionable video-game players dedicated to publishing great graphic novels for all ages. I'm Jim Salicrup, Editor-in-Chief , and I hope you enjoyed this all-new graphic novel, written by Tini Howard, and illustrated by Jules Rivera, inspired by the DVD starring Barbie, and featuring Chelsea, Crystal, Cutie, Gaia, Kris, Maia, Princess Bella, Renee, and Teresa .

If BARBIE VIDEO GAME HERO was your very first BARBIE graphic novel, and you enjoyed it, we have good news for you! There are several other BARBIE graphic novels from Papercutz available at your favorite bookseller or library that you may enjoy as well...

The first graphic novel is BARBIE #1 "Fashion Superstar," by Sarah Kuhn, writer, and Alitha Martinez, artist. Barbie dreams of a career in fashion, and she just got her first big break—assisting world-famous fashion designer Whitney Yang at her big Spring Fashion Show! But when things start going wrong, it's up to Barbie and her friends to work some fashion miracles.

In BARBIE #2 "Big Dreams, Best Friends," by Sarah Kuhn, writer, and Yishan Li, artist. Barbie continues on her fashion adventure, this time designing for one of the world's biggest pop stars. But when Barbie experiences designer's block and can't get in the stitch of things, helping out the shy drummer may get her back on track!

BARBIE PUPPY PARTY, by Danica Davidson, writer, and Maria Victoria Robado, artist. Not only does it star Barbie, it also features Barbie's sisters, Chelsea, Stacie, and Skipper, along with their pet puppies, Honey, Rookie, Taffy, and DJ! Barbie and her sisters are organizing an adoption event for the local animal shelter, but it's scheduled on the same day as the puppies' birthday. The Puppies think they're being forgotten, but that can't be, can it? The surprising answer awaits you within BARBIE PUPPY PARTY.

In BARBIE STAR LIGHT ADVENTURE, by Tini Howard, writer, and Jules Rivera, artist, the same creative team who brought you BARBIE VIDEO GAME HERO, Barbie, in this special graphic novel, is Princess Star Light, from the planet Para-Den. When she discovers someone is trying to destroy the environment, Barbie and her friends, Sal-Lee (a hoverboard racing legend), Sheena and Kareena (Gravity Geniuses), and Leo (Prince and pilot) work together to save the planet they love.

And there are more great BARBIE graphic novels to come! We don't want you to miss out on any of the great BARBIE comics, so for more news about upcoming BARBIE graphic novels, be sure to visit Papercutz.com.

Thanks,

JIM

STAY IN TOUCH!

EMAIL: salicrup@papercutz.com
WEB: papercutz.com
INSTAGRAM: @papercutzgn
TWITTER: @papercutzgn
FACEBOOK: PAPERCUTZGRAPHICNOVELS
FANMAIL: Papercutz, 160 Broadway, Suite 700
             East Wing, New York, NY 10038

58

...NEAR THE BOTTOM OF THE DRESS.

OOOH, *LOVE IT!*

I HAVE AN IDEA FOR THAT, CHRISTINE, I CAN DO SOME OF MY *TRADEMARK FABRIC DRAPING*...

MAYBE YOU CAN COME UP WITH SOMETHING COOL LIKE THAT FOR *DREA*, MY *NEW DRUMMER.* SHE JUST JOINED THE BAND AND HAS NEVER BEEN ON A *MAJOR TOUR* BEFORE...

THAT'S RIGHT, LIZ. HER DRUMMING IS *DAZZLING* IN REHEARSAL, WHEN THERE'S NO ONE ELSE AROUND.

YOUR TOUR MANAGER SAID SHE WAS HAVING *STAGE FRIGHT?*

BUT PUT HER IN FRONT OF A CROWD AND SHE JUST *FREEZES UP*...OR DRUMS TOO HARD AND *LOSES THE RHYTHM*...

ANYWAY, I'M SURE THE *EXCITEMENT* WILL TAKE OVER ONCE THE TOUR *TRULY STARTS* AND SHE'LL BE FINE! SHE IS THE MOST *TALENTED DRUMMER* I'VE EVER KNOWN!

SO, WHITNEY, LET'S GET THIS DRESS *FIXED UP!*

GO WAIT FOR ME IN YOUR DRESSING ROOM--I'LL BE *RIGHT THERE!*

BARBIE, YOU WEREN'T HIRED FOR THIS TOUR JUST TO ASSIST ME WITH *MY DESIGNS*-- CHRISTINE WANTS *YOUR VISION*, TOO.

I DON'T KNOW IF I CAN FIND IT.

YOU JUST NEED SOMETHING TO *FOCUS ON.*

WHY DON'T YOU DESIGN ONE *SUPER COOL ACCESSORY* FOR A BAND MEMBER? SOMETHING THAT SHOWCASES YOUR *SIGNATURE FLAIR.*

OH! DO .OU REALLY THIN' THAT WILL HEI. '?

OF COURSE IT WILL! IT'S LIKE WHAT CHRISTINE WAS SAYING ABOUT DREA: THE EXCITEMENT OF THE TOUR WILL TAKE OVER AND YOU'LL *ROCK IT OUT!*

AND REMEMBER: WE'RE *HERE FOR YOU!*

YES! I'M SO *THRILLED* I GOT TO COME WITH YOU GUYS AND COVER THE TOUR FOR THE *STYLE LOVE BLOG!* WE'RE GOING TO HAVE THE *MOST FUN!*

AND YOU WILL FIND *YOUR VISION* AGAIN!

Don't Miss Barbie #2 available now!

THE STORY OF *Barbie* ™

AND THE WOMAN WHO CREATED HER

On Sale 9/5/17

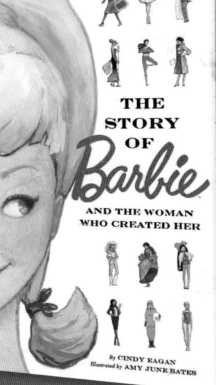

THE STORY OF *Barbie* ™

AND THE WOMAN WHO CREATED HER

By CINDY EAGAN
Illustrated by AMY JUNE BATES

Discover the true story of the world's most famous doll.

RHCB

Visit BarbieBooks.com to order your copy!